EARTHQUAKE

BY MATT CHRISTOPHER

ILLUSTRATED BY
TED LEWIN

Little, Brown and Company
BOSTON   TORONTO

FIRST EDITION

T 11/75

Library of Congress Cataloging in Publication Data

Christopher, Matthew F
  Earthquake.

  SUMMARY: After running away from camp in the Adiron-dack Mountains on his horse, Jeff encounters unimaginable ordeals, including a severe earthquake.
  [1. Runaways—Fiction]. 2. Earthquakes—Fiction]
I. Lewin, Ted. II. Title.
PZ7.C458Ear   [Fic]   75-22153
ISBN 0-316-13968-8

Published simultaneously in Canada
by Little, Brown & Company (Canada) Limited

PRINTED IN THE UNITED STATES OF AMERICA

AUTHOR'S NOTE

Although there actually have been earthquakes in the Adirondack Mountains of New York State, where this story takes place, the earthquake described in this book is purely imaginary.

The Blue Fox Search and Rescue teams of Region 6 are real, but any similarity of names used in the story to actual persons, living or dead, is purely coincidental.

To the people who so kindly supplied me with the information I needed about search and rescue, and about earthquakes in New York State, I am humbly grateful.

EARTHQUAKE

ONE

It started far below the surface of the earth — a huge rupturing. Slowly it began to spread, sending out vibrations. A giant was awakening from a long sleep.

Muscles bulged under his red velvet hide. His long copper-colored tail snapped like a whip. The chestnut horse, Red, lifted his front legs and brought them down gently upon the graveled creek bank.

Jeff Belno, holding firmly onto the reins, looked back beyond the narrow creek that ribboned through the valley of trees behind him.

Camp Ga-wan-da and Pointed Rock Pond were out of sight.

His escape route was through the mountains. He would be followed, he was sure of that, even though here at the creek his trail would disappear. It would take an expert guide to track him down in that leaf-carpeted, overgrown jungle.

"Okay, Red. Across the creek," Jeff said, pulling gently on the left rein.

Red's nostrils flared, and he snorted as he stepped into the creek. The water was clear, and it flowed swiftly, rising up over his legs as he started to walk gingerly across. By the time he reached the middle of the stream, the water was up to his hocks.

Suddenly his right front leg slipped, and Jeff felt a moment of panic. He tightened his legs against Red's belly.

"Careful, Red!" he said.

He had expected hazardous moments. Not one inch of the long journey was going to be easy. He had thought about it a lot during his waking hours, and even during sleep, too, when he had dreamed about the journey. Creeks, dotted with hidden, slippery rocks; deep ravines; steep, treacherous gorges. They were all there — some-

4

where. He'd meet them, sooner or later. And who was he counting on to get through them or over them, one way or another? Red. His big, faithful, beautiful horse, Red.

He had had Red for almost all of two years, having raised him since just a few days after the colt's birth. Red had been a gift to Jeff on his birthday from his Uncle Bob, his mother's brother in Ohio. Jeff played with Red and talked to him as he would to a brother.

Jeff's sister, Patty Marie, loved Red, too. But her love didn't go as deep as Jeff's did. Red was his horse. His alone.

At last the big chestnut trudged out of the creek and onto the hard rocky shore. Jeff gave a final glance up the creek, then rode on.

The morning sun blinded him momentarily as it started its slow climb up over the trees, striking the water with golden flashes of light. A chipmunk skittered across the path in front of them and scrambled up a tree. A songbird chirped its melodious song from the top of a nearby spruce and was answered by its mate from another. The farther up the mountain Jeff rode, the more evident were the sounds of birds and animals as they began their day.

Jeff reined in Red and listened for any sounds besides those of the wildlife around him. He was sure that by now his and Red's absence from camp would have been discovered. And they — Norman Dorg, the camp director, and the sixty-odd boys at the camp — would know immediately that he had run away.

Mr. Dorg would waste no time in picking a handful of the biggest boys and starting a wide, intensive search. He would lead his party far into the mountains, determined to search until he found the runaway boy and his horse, or until he had to give up for fear of getting lost.

Here in the Adirondacks, the largest mountains in New York State, even experienced hunters had often ventured too far and gotten lost. Sometimes they were found, nearly dead from exposure and starvation. Sometimes they were not found at all.

Already Jeff felt the fear of loneliness, and of losing his way, even though he had a compass and a map. But he had to make the journey. He had planned this escape for two whole days, having made up his mind that running away was his only choice. He was determined not to take the humiliation from Norman Dorg any longer.

"Belno! Who told you to put out a fire by step-ping on it?"

Jeff looked at him, his eyes wide and anxious. "There are just two sticks left, sir."

"I don't care if there's just one teeny-weeny stick!" Norman Dorg barked. "You're going to put that fire out with dirt!"

"Yes, sir," said Jeff, and he ran to the toolshed for the shovel.

One of the kids behind him laughed.

"Okay, Mitchell!" Norman Dorg snapped. "You go with him and bring the pitchfork!"

Nobody laughed then.

During most of his young life Jeff had known that he wasn't as smart as a lot of kids. Two years ago he had been put back from the fifth grade to the fourth, and since then he had managed to hold his own. But he knew he was a slow learner. Man, how well he knew. Mrs. Dunning, his teacher, had reminded him of it at least a dozen times in that painful, formidable way of hers.

"Jeff, aren't you *ever* going to learn?" It wasn't only what she said; it was that awful tone she used.

And how many times had his mother and

father and Patty Marie reminded him he was slow? Especially Patty Marie, who sometimes was as bad as Norman Dorg. But he could take it from her more easily than from the camp coach, because he wasn't afraid to dish it back to her.

It was different with Norman Dorg. If Jeff had talked back to him, Dorg would have punished him somehow, he was sure of it. Jeff had never seen Dorg punish anybody physically. Cutting a kid down with his kind of sarcasm was punishment enough.

He had no watch, but he was sure it was around noontime when the sun reached its zenith and his stomach cried of hunger.

He found an open clearing just large enough for Red and himself to lie down in to eat and rest. They interrupted a mother rabbit and her three young ones, nibbling on a small clump of grass. The rabbits hesitated just long enough to see who the newcomers were, then sprang off into the woods.

Jeff chuckled as he slid down off Red. He was reminded of the white rabbits he and Patty Marie were raising. They had six, three males and three

8

females. In about two weeks one of them, Dolly, would be giving birth to her litter.

He removed the rucksack from his back, then sat down on a carpet of dried leaves, his back against a tree. He opened it, took out and unwrapped a bar of candy, and tossed it to Red. Gracefully the horse leaned down, picked it up with his teeth and began to chew it.

Then Jeff took out a sandwich and bit into it. Unfortunately, he had no Thermos, nothing that held any juices or water. That was his greatest worry at the moment; he knew they couldn't go too far without water. By nightfall he would have to find a spring or creek.

A new sound came from somewhere in the distance. Jeff paused, the sandwich half eaten.

It was the sound of a low-flying airplane. Probably Norman Dorg's. He had a two-seater Aeronca Champion which he kept on the same field where Jeff had kept Red. A flying buff, Dorg hadn't missed a day of spending at least an hour or so in the sky. It was probably him in his plane, searching for Jeff.

Jeff felt his chest tighten as he looked up at the patch of clear blue sky visible through the tops of the trees. Then he glanced at Red standing in direct sunlight, completely innocent of what was going on.

"Oh, man!" Jeff cried as he laid the sandwich aside and sprang to his feet. "If that's Norman Dorg and he sees us, we're licked!"

TWO

The vibrations, slight at first, intensified by the second. It would be a while before they reached the surface.

Jeff grabbed the reins and pulled his horse under the trees, staying with him while his heart pounded like a drum.

He heard the plane coming closer and closer, and then heard it flying almost directly overhead. He looked up, but the branches and pine needles were thick and in his way.

After several minutes the sound of the airplane faded into the distance, but Jeff stayed in his spot until some ten minutes after he had last heard the

sound. Then he hurried across the clearing, picked up the remnants of his sandwich, and finished it.

He got another one out of his rucksack and gave it to Red. Then he mounted the horse, grabbed the reins, and dug his heels in gently. Red started off, his plumelike tail snapping to scare off a black fly. The fly buzzed off and landed on Jeff's neck. Jeff swatted it, picked it off his skin, and disgustedly flicked it away.

The appearance of the little pest made him shudder. The black fly, about one-tenth the size of the common housefly, was one of the worst nuisances of the mountains. Its bites left welts which were sometimes the size of golf balls. Jeff had never forgotten the swelling his father had gotten from one a couple of years ago when he had gone to the mountains on a fishing trip.

An hour or so later Jeff spotted a white-tailed deer peering curiously at them from behind a low bush ahead. It sported a rack of antlers, and a thrill swept through Jeff as it always did when he saw a wild deer.

"Look at him, Red," he whispered. "Isn't he a beauty?"

A moment later the animal turned and bounded away, its white tail flashing for just an instant before it disappeared.

As he rode on, Jeff started thinking about water again. Then he realized that he really wasn't that thirsty. *I wonder why?* he asked himself. Well, he had eaten only one sandwich, for one thing. The less he ate, the less water he required. He had to remember that. The same applied to Red. But Red was burning up his energy. Food and water could not be denied him for long.

Soon they came to a flat, partially open stretch and a sight which sickened Jeff. Tall, blackened stalks stood as ugly reminders of a fire that must have taken place some years back. Jeff reflected that it had probably been started by either a careless hunter who had failed to quench his campfire completely, or by lightning.

Will people ever wise up? thought Jeff. *Will they ever learn to think when they go out hunting, fishing, or just simply camping to get away from civilization for a while?*

A group of crows cawed as they left the branches of a tree not too far from Jeff, and in their slow, unhurried way they flew across the

skeletal forest and landed on one of the blackened stumps.

Here again both Red and Jeff became bothered by the obnoxious black flies, and quickly hastened into the shelter of the green woods.

Once far enough away, Jeff reined Red in, dismounted, and dug into his rucksack for his map. He unrolled it and located Camp Ga-wan-da, which he had circled in red. Then he looked at a line he had drawn with a pencil between Pointed Rock Pond, where Camp Ga-wan-da was situated, and Dory Mills, his home. He took out the compass, laid the map as flat as he could on the ground, and placed the compass on it, turning it so that the needle pointed directly north.

He had read about compass variation, the difference between true north and the magnetic pole. An airplane pilot's map, or a mariner's chart, usually included a diagram showing how to calculate for the degrees of variation. Jeff's map had no such diagram, but he had an idea of how to compensate for the difference. He turned the compass so that the needle pointed five degrees to the left of north. This wasn't accurate, but it would get him fairly close to home, provided rough terrain didn't force him too far off his course.

It was hard for Jeff to determine how far he had come, but he didn't think it was more than five miles. As the crow flies, that meant that he had about thirty more miles to go. Since he was traveling by horse, he had to add at least five more miles to that. Perhaps ten. According to the map there were Rich Lake, Wolf Pond, and Cold River to get around one way or another before another long stretch home.

He looked up through the trees and suddenly noticed, by the darkening shadows, that the sun was setting. He got a little scared as he looked ahead to nightfall and sleeping in the mountains. Thank heaven Red was with him.

But without Red would he really have attempted this long, perilous journey?

No, of course not.

No way.

He wasn't crazy, for Pete's sake.

He dropped the compass into his pants pocket, returned the map to the rucksack, and strapped the rucksack to his back. Then he mounted Red again and continued on his way, finding that the trailless woods were more dense with brush and trees than he had expected.

He had hoped to reach Rich Lake before dark,

but as it turned out he didn't. He tried not to let it bother him as he looked for a suitable spot where he and Red could sleep for the night.

"Here's a nice little space, Red," he said as he found a clearing under a giant spruce. "It's not like a motel where we can watch TV till all hours of the night, but what can we expect for nothing? Right?"

He reined the horse to a halt, dismounted, took off his rucksack, then loosened the cinch of Red's saddle.

"There you are," he said. "Bet that began to feel like a girdle on you after a day like this." He chuckled as he patted Red's head, then pressed his cheek gently against it. "We'll make it all right, Red. You'll see."

But I am worried, he thought. *This trip isn't as easy as I had figured it would be. Not that I had thought it would be simple.*

He gave Red half a peanut butter sandwich and ate the other half himself. Then he pulled out a liverwurst sandwich, and considered splitting it between them the same way. The horse looked at him, then at the sandwich with wide, imploring eyes, and a grin came over Jeff's face.

"You didn't think for one minute that I'd want

a part of that, did you?" he said, chuckling as he held out both halves.

As daintily as he was able, Red removed one half the sandwich from Jeff's palm, chewed it, swallowed it, then repeated the process with the second half.

"I know you could eat a lot more than that, Red," Jeff said, regretfully. "But all I have left are four more sandwiches. We've got to take it easy."

Red gazed straight ahead, with big, innocent eyes. His tail swished.

"Sorry, Red," said Jeff. "That's the way it has to be till something different turns up."

Even though Jeff knew Red could not understand what he was saying, talking to his horse took the edge off the loneliness of the mountains, the quiet that lay everywhere like a haunting, heavy presence.

THREE

The vibrations not only moved outward, like the ripples in a pond after a stone had been thrown into it: they moved upward, too, toward the earth's surface.

In Watertown, headquarters for the Blue Fox Search and Rescue teams of Region 6, the red telephone rang on the desk of District Forest Ranger Tom Murray. He picked it up.

"Tom Murray here."

"Tom, this is Dave Watkins. Just got a call from a Norman Dorg, head of the Ga-wan-da Boys' Camp on Pointed Rock Pond. One of the boys ran away from camp on a horse."

"A horse?"

"That's right . . . a horse. The kid had taken it with him to camp. Don't ask me why. Anyway, Dorg had done some searching on his own by air. He's got an Aeronca Champ. But no luck. He's sure the kid doesn't want to be found."

Tom shook his head. What kind of kid would want to do a crazy thing like that?

"Must have really liked camp," he said.

"Yeah. The kid's name is Jeff Belno and his home is in Dory Mills."

"That's pretty far north of where the camp is, isn't it?"

"Right. Anyway, it's possible that he might be heading in that direction. Dorg thinks the kid's carrying a compass, but doesn't claim the kid as one of his smartest."

"Strike two," said Tom dismally. No one — not even an adult — could claim smartness if he thought he could challenge the remote regions of the Adirondacks alone.

"Well, you've got the ball," Dave finished. "Carry it through, and let me know if you scored a touchdown. Okay?"

"Right, Dave."

"Good luck."

"We may need it. Ten four," said Tom, and jabbed a finger on the receiver button to break the connection. A moment later he dialed another number.

"Lou," said Tom when he heard the low, familiar voice of Lou Aldon, the Operations Supervisor stationed near the Pointed Rock Pond area. "This is Tom Murray. We may have a big one on our hands. A kid ran away from Camp Ga-wan-da on his horse."

Seconds after Tom put down the phone the wheels of the Search and Rescue teams went into motion. Five teams of ten forest rangers and a leader each headed for a rendezvous at Camp Ga-wan-da. Staying with a four-wheel-drive van parked as close to the mountainous slope as it could get, Lou Aldon watched the men take off on foot in the direction assumed to have been taken by Jeff. All they had to work on at the moment was the general direction in which the boy's home lay — north-northwest.

In the van was all the essential equipment needed for any kind of emergency: first-aid kit, snakebite kit, protractor, chain saw, climbers, shovels, axes, lights, grappling irons, rope.

And, constantly, with Lou, was the two-way radio.

An extensive, and an intensive, search for young Jeff Belno had begun.

It rained during the night. Forks of lightning pierced the sky, followed by crashes of thunder. Rain pelted the trees, driven by gusts of a wind that whistled and howled like some giant, invisible animal. Jeff woke up and snuggled against Red's back, protected only by the rucksack, which barely covered his shoulders.

"I hadn't figured on this, Red," he said softly. "Otherwise I would've brought a raincoat or something. You're lucky," he went on, shivering from the cold that was starting to creep in through his clothes. "You've got a thick hide to keep yourself warm."

He fell silent, and almost instantly his thoughts roamed to home — to his parents and his sister, Patty Marie. But mostly they centered on his father — tall, rawboned, friendly but firm John Belno, who ruled the household on important matters and, quite often, on minor ones, too. What would he say when he heard that his son had broken away from camp? How could Jeff make him believe that he just could not tolerate Norman Dorg's humiliation and iron rule any longer? Was that really reason enough, John Belno might think, for Jeff to run away?

He dove into the water from the four-feet-high diving board and began the long seventy-five-yard swim across the pond. He knew he would never make it. He hadn't swum more than ten or fifteen yards in his life.

He had barely covered a third of the distance when his arms and legs began to tire. When he was halfway across his limbs felt as if they were ready to drop off.

"Come on! Rest a few seconds, then move on!" Norman Dorg yelled from shore. "You can do it!"

He rested. What else could he do? Then he gasped for breath, and looked at the two kids in the rowboat some twenty yards away. They were unaware of his predicament, thinking about their own fun and nothing else.

He started to go down. His head went under. Moving his arms and legs frantically — and, oh, how they ached! — he rose to the surface, spat out a mouthful of water, and sucked in a lungful of air.

"Jim! Butch!" Norman Dorg yelled to the kids in the boat. "Pick up Jeff! Hurry!"

Jeff shuddered as the horrible memory passed through his mind. Norman Dorg had to see him at the brink of death before ordering those kids to rescue him.

He realized he was wide awake now, and wondered what time it was. Two o'clock? Four? He noticed that dawn was breaking through the trees. It was that eerie early-morning hour when shadows began to take shape.

Another bright streak of lightning lit up the forest. In that brief instant he caught a glimpse of something standing in the clearing across from him. Whatever it was — an animal or a human being — blended with the foliage that surrounded it.

Jeff shuddered. Its eyes were trained directly on him.

FOUR

The energy released by the vibrations was building. It was rising up into the heart of the Adirondack Mountains.

He could barely hear the sounds it made — they were muffled by the wind and thunder — but he could see the shape of the thing. It was large and round, with legs.

A bear?

He sprang to his feet, just as another streak of lightning lit up the trees and the clearing. This time there was no doubt about it. It was a bear. A black, full-grown, monstrous-looking bear.

In that brief moment he had glimpsed something else, too. There was another bear with the first one, but this one was much smaller. It was a cub.

Oh, man! Jeff thought. *The last things in the world I wanted to come across are a mother bear and her cub!*

He slid on a carpet of pine needles as he tried to scramble to his feet. He felt awkward, clumsy and scared. The closest he'd ever been to a bear was at a park where a high wire fence separated the animals from the visitors. That was the best way — the safest way — to look at a bear.

Right now, though, there was nothing between him and the bears but an empty space and a patch of darkness that lit up intermittently as lightning forked across the sky. He had read articles about bears, had seen them in movies where they appeared to be balls of fur with only one thing in mind — play.

Oh, sure!

The black bear could be a cheerful, quiet animal, but it could also be treacherous. And the black bear cub could be the most dangerous.

Never trust them! the article warned.

Jeff flung the rucksack over his shoulder and rushed to his horse.

Red was already on his feet, staring wildly in the direction of the animals.

Jeff grabbed the reins, swung his right leg up over Red, then looked back at the bears. He was about to dig his heels into Red's ribs, but he paused when he thought he was going to be treated to an unusual sight. The mother bear had suddenly decided to investigate a beechnut tree for nuts. But then the tree quickly seemed to lose its appeal for the bear, and Jeff wondered if it was because it was too slim to climb. He had heard that although bears climbed trees, they preferred them to be at least a foot in diameter to give their claws plenty of bark to grip.

Even though both bears seemed oblivious of the boy and horse, their closeness worried Jeff. Better to get away from them right now, he decided.

Lightning pierced the sky again, followed by a boom of thunder, as Jeff rode on through the mountains. All at once rain poured down, pelting the swaying branches. They were poor umbrellas, offering some protection, but not much.

After a while Jeff forgot about the bears. By now he figured that he must have ridden close to a mile, far enough to prevent his and the bears' paths from crossing again.

He was soaked to the skin. *If Mom saw me now*, he thought, *she'd scalp me.*

He thought about what he was doing, and felt a sense of guilt. But, should he? he asked himself. Should he feel guilty for running away? Wasn't his reason justified?

I don't care what anybody thinks, he told himself firmly. *I know I did the right thing. I know.*

Suddenly, he felt a pang as he thought about camp and some of the games played there. Touch tackle, softball, volley ball. The only trouble was that he never got to play as much as he would have liked. It was the old theme: the survival of the fittest. The better players played the most. He wasn't in their league. He played some, because every kid who wanted to, played. Chalk up one good point for Norman Dorg. It was one of his iron rules. *"I don't want any kid going home saying he never played anything!"*

Eventually, the rain stopped.

"Hold it, Red," Jeff said, pulling gently on the reins.

Red halted, and Jeff looked up through the trees. The sky was visible in jagged patches of pink and blue, like the pieces of a puzzle. Though he felt no breeze, he could see the leaves stirring ever so slightly, as if they were breathing. A drop of rain splashed on his cheek, and he blinked. He saw he was surrounded by close-cropped trees and brush. Snakelike vines extended in various directions like the long tentacles of some kind of prehistoric octopus.

The Adirondacks? It was more like the jungles of Africa!

A chill rippled through him in one violent shudder, a combination of his soaked clothes and the feeling of being caught in a trap. In that single moment he felt that he would never see his mother and father and sister again, or any other human being. They all seemed trillions of miles away, or on another planet. Tears burned his eyes then, and a lump rose in his throat that felt ready to burst.

He gripped the reins tightly to suppress the crying that wanted to come. Holding back tears would be a victory he needed now.

He closed his mouth and pressed his teeth together and held his breath. Gradually the lump in his throat melted. He blinked away the few tears that blurred his eyes and wiped them with the back of his hand.

He was over the hump now. He had won.

He took a deep breath, then got the map and compass out of the rucksack. Good thing he had checked — he had been riding too far westward, he noticed.

But to get out of here meant some clever maneuvering. And to follow the direction indicated by the compass needle meant that Red would have to plough through a maze of vines and tangled bushes.

He directed Red around the bush and trees and flushed out a family of rabbits that startled both him and his horse. Then he headed almost straight eastward for about twenty feet before there was a clearing he could take that led northwestward.

He rode steadily, with a glance now and then at the compass, for the route now was more erratic than before.

Little by little the last shadows of night lifted, and the warm, sparkling colors of the leaves and bushes brightened the forest. Seeing broad daylight again erased most of the fear that the rainy night and the sight of the bears had instilled in Jeff, but not all. He wasn't quite used to the early morning sounds yet: the chittering squirrels, the whistling birds, the silences that came in between.

He came to a spot where a shaft of sunlight blazed through the trees like a golden spear, and there he stood for a while to let the sun dry his clothes. Its warmth felt good. Almost suddenly he felt a joy about being where he was and doing what he was doing. Never had he been so free in his life, nor had he seen such sights. Yes, he would keep forever the memory of the bears.

And, man, he had barely started! There was so much farther to go!

He was tired, hungry; he had slept very little during the night. After a while he took a sandwich out of his rucksack and split it with Red. The morsel hardly filled the empty pit in his stomach, but he'd hold off before he would have anymore.

In the dense forest that lay north of Pointed Rock Pond the Search and Rescue teams sent out to find Jeff Belno weren't having any luck. They had hoped to find the boy's trail before it rained last night, but they hadn't. They had been look- ing for anything Jeff might have left behind — a sandwich wrapper, anything — but they had found nothing. That suggested that either he was a cautious, alert kid, or that they just weren't heading in the right direction.

Now, this morning, their hopes of finding a trail were diminished to almost zero. Last night's rain could have washed away any telltale sign that either the boy or his horse had left.

Mark Taylor, a twenty-two-year-old, country-raised leader of one of the teams, signaled to his men to stop in their search only long enough for him to dispatch a report to the Operations Supervisor, Lou Aldon. "Lou, Mark Taylor. Nothing so far. That rain didn't help matters, either."

"I know," answered Lou. "Did your boys make it through the night without getting too wet?"

"Those pup tents came in handy," Mark replied.

"They always do. Okay, Mark. Keep looking. Ten four."

FIVE

The movement was rising higher and higher, like a boil.

Jeff jerked the reins, pulling Red to a stop. "Hold it, Red," he whispered.

He saw the eyes first. They were shining like balls of silver as the sun hit them. Then he saw the long muzzle, the head, and — partially hidden by leaves — the rack of antlers.

"Well, good morning," Jeff greeted the buck deer warmly. "And how are you . . . ?"

Before Jeff was able to finish his greeting, the deer's ears quivered. Then he turned and disappeared almost instantly behind the trees, letting

Jeff have just a fleeting glimpse of his bobbing, white-tipped tail.

Now that he had stopped briefly, Jeff decided to check his map and compass a little more thoroughly this time. After spending almost two minutes on the map, he turned the compass so that the needle pointed in the direction he wanted to go, then got moving again.

The earth was softer here, and with each step Red's hooves sank in the damp carpet of dead leaves. A clean, fresh smell permeated the air, and, except for his clothes that still felt slightly damp, and a gnawing, hungry ache in his stomach, Jeff felt good.

After riding for a couple of hours Jeff arrived at the brink of a cliff. His heart sang as he gazed down at the waters of a slow-moving river.

"It's water, Red!" he cried happily. "It's water!"

His throat and tongue were dry as paper.

Glad that so far he was heading in the right direction, he let out a whoop of joy and guided Red along the edge of the cliff down to the graveled shore. It wasn't till then that he saw the real color of the water. It was brown, dirtied from the mud washed down by last night's rain.

Sick with disappointment, he sat there while Red approached the water and began to drink.

"I suppose it won't hurt you," Jeff said. "But I'm going to boil it for me."

He got down, and proceeded to gather pieces of wood to build a fire. With his knife he whittled three short pieces so that curly shavings stuck out from all around them. He placed these in a pile, got out his small box of matches and, striking one of them, ignited the wood. Then he put on larger pieces and soon had a fire blazing.

He waited till the wood burned down to coals. Then he filled up the flat aluminum pan, the only utensil he had in the rucksack, with water, and placed it on the hot coals. He let it boil what he guessed were fifteen to twenty minutes. Then he placed the pan in the water to cool, waited another fifteen to twenty minutes, and tasted it. It was warm, and flat; but at least he felt safe in knowing that it wasn't contaminated.

He gave Red a sandwich and had one himself. Then he sat with his back against a boulder while he waited for a second pan of water to boil.

A sound made him sit bolt upright. He listened hard. It was the chop-chopping noise of a helicopter! Norman Dorg must have notified the police and now *they* were searching for him!

Leaping to his feet, he dumped the pan of water onto the fire. Then he got more water and poured it on the flames. Quickly he pushed the remains of the fire into the river, then grabbed Red's reins and drew him into the woods.

A minute later the chopping sound came from almost directly above. Jeff tried to peer through the trees, but they were so thick he could hardly see the sky.

Breathlessly he waited. By the sound of the 'copter's motor and whipping blades, he could tell that it had changed its course and was following the river northward.

Good thinking, Jeff reflected with a smile — except that following the river wasn't the course he had planned on. If he had wanted to be found, staying by the river would be the sensible thing to do. But being rescued was the last thing he wanted. Norman Dorg would show him what punishment really was if he were picked up now.

After a while the sound of the helicopter died

away, but Jeff waited for about another fifteen minutes before moving on. What he had to look for now was a narrow, shallow part of the river.

He must have ridden two miles before he eventually found a neck in the river that looked reasonably safe enough to cross. The distance across was about sixty feet, broken by large, protruding rocks. A closer look, though, made him reconsider. The water definitely flowed faster here; white froth in the eddies was a sure sign of it.

Jeff looked up the river as far as he could. Ahead it was wider, and filled with rapids. Now he was sure this spot was the best place to cross.

But how deep was it? It was impossible to tell from the water's muddiness.

Somewhere ahead, though, beyond that clump of forest, was a lake. He had to find it, and then camp for a while on its north shore.

Gripping the reins tightly, he urged Red into the water. Timidly, Red stepped in and started to cross.

With each step the water got deeper. When they were about half way across, the water was up to Red's belly and covering Jeff's feet.

Fear began taking hold of Jeff. The roar of the

water rushing around the rocks was a steady rumble that began to sound more and more threatening. He realized now that it was more dangerous than he had expected.

But Red would make it. Jeff was sure of it.

"Keep going, Red," he said, his voice soft and encouraging. "You're doing fine."

Red took another step — and another. Suddenly he slipped and fell, and the swift water rushed over him.

Eyes wide with panic, Jeff sprang free of the horse. He sank, then bolted to the surface, stroking and kicking with all the power he could muster. He felt the rucksack strike a boulder, then heard the sound of tearing cloth.

Spitting out water that had filled his mouth, and putting out his hands to keep from being driven against another boulder, he saw the rucksack disappear in a swirling eddy, appear again, then float away on the swift current.

SIX

It was inevitable. Nothing would stop it.

Dory Mills was a quiet little town near the St. Regis River and some ten miles west of St. Regis Falls. The thousands of acres of land surrounding it were known for their scenic splendor. Popular fishing and hunting grounds attracted outdoor enthusiasts from all over the state.

In one of the town's older homes situated close to the edge of the woods, John Belno had just hung up the telephone. His hand shook slightly as he raised it to his head and swept back a stubborn tuft of black hair.

It was 7:05 A.M. In five more minutes he had intended to leave for work.

"John!" his wife exclaimed, staring at him. "Your face is white as a sheet! Who was that?"

A tall man, almost too thin, because of a diabetic condition, he sat down on a chair before he answered her. "Norm . . ." He cleared his throat. "Norman Dorg."

The concern in Ann Belno's deep blue eyes intensified.

"Norman Dorg? Isn't he the director at the boys' camp?"

Her husband nodded. "Yes. He said that Jeff ran away last night. He took off on Red."

"What?" A furrow deepened in her forehead. "Why would he do that?"

"I don't know. But you know Jeff. He's — different than most boys. Something didn't go right."

She seemed to melt as she sat at the table opposite him. "I didn't think he'd run away, no matter what happened there," she whispered huskily.

Her husband was staring through the window, but what he saw were images of his son: Jeff immersed in an animal book; building a tree house in the backyard on his own; riding in the hills on Red. He was a loner, but he rarely showed signs of unhappiness. No friends ever called at the house, although sometimes he would accept an invitation to go to someone else's house. His only real close friend was his horse, Red.

"Something happened, all right," John Belno said, "or he wouldn't have run away."

"Do you suppose that he got into a hassle with some of the kids?" Ann said.

"Hard to tell," replied John. "I just remember, though, what Tom Botner said to me before the boys left on the bus and you and I drove off with Red in the van."

"What did he say?"

"Well, it was what young Tommy had told him. Tommy had been at the camp the year before, and he didn't seem especially happy about going again. He said that Norman Dorg was very strict, and treated some of the boys as if they were in an army camp."

"That must have stuck in Jeff's mind," said Ann.

"Right. And that's probably why he wanted to have Red down there with him, not just to ride him now and then as he said. Maybe he sort of

44

expected something to happen between him and Dorg, and took the easy way out — ran away."

"Oh, John. He's a very sensitive boy. Easily hurt."

"I know. I know."

She glanced at the wall clock with anxious eyes. "About what time did they say Jeff left?"

"Sometime after supper last night. Dorg searched for him for a while in his own airplane, then called the Search and Rescue people."

"They saw no sign of him?"

"None."

She got up and went into the other room, her legs unsteady. John watched her go. She was a delicate woman, but during the sixteen years of their marriage he had never known her to shy away from any problem, no matter how serious it was. This anxiety over Jeff was beginning to loom larger than any he could remember. If Jeff was going through the mountains with Red — and all signs seem to indicate that he was — he would be encountering some of the most dangerous terrain that existed in the Adirondacks: steep hills, gullies, rocks, cliffs, swift-flowing rivers, lakes, and — not to be ignored — wildcats and bears.

Anger rushed to his throat and then subsided, as love and concern for his son won him over. He stood up as Ann came back into the room, her eyes red now.

"What are we going to do?" she asked, wiping away her tears with a handkerchief.

"What can we do? I have a hunch that what Jeff did was head in this direction. He took a compass and a map with him to camp, you remember. He may be slow, but he's no dumbbell."

The back door opened and slammed shut. A young girl of fourteen ran into the house, her patched blue jeans tight as a glove around her slim legs. Last night she had stayed with her friend, Mary Ann Colter, four houses away.

She stopped on the threshhold between the kitchen and the living room and stared at her parents. Her cheeks were white and her eyes were big and round.

"Mom! Dad! Did you hear about Jeff? It just came over the radio! He's run away from camp!"

"Dad just got a call from Mr. Dorg, the camp director," her mother said in a strained voice. "Was there anything else said?"

"Just that an air search was being made for

him," the girl answered. She went to a chair, sat down and buried her head in her arms.

Her mother went to her, and put her arms tenderly around her shoulders. Patty Marie, a year and a half older than Jeff, was their only daughter. She had often said in front of Jeff that she wished she had a sister instead of a brother. A "dumb brother" was the way she had sometimes put it. Often her mother, or her father, would warn her about it when Jeff wasn't around. Although she would promise not to say it again, she would sometimes forget, and "you dumbbell" would pop out of her mouth before she could restrain herself.

John stood and picked up the phone. He called the personnel office at the place where he worked.

"Josie? This is John Belno. Give Ed Jason a message for me, will you? Tell him I won't be in today."

The rushing water thrust Jeff down into an eddy, spinning him like a top. He managed to struggle out of it, and suddenly found himself being carried like a log down the fast-moving current. He kept his head above water, kicking and stroking with all his might.

At long last, almost when he felt he could not stay afloat another second, his hands and feet touched rock. He pulled himself up and crawled to shore, panting so hard his lungs ached. He became dizzy. His head buzzed, and flashes of light danced before his eyes. Once on dry ground, he collapsed.

He lay there for several minutes while his head cleared and he regained his strength. Then he raised his head and looked around for Red.

Where was he, anyway?

He hasn't gone into the woods looking for me, has he? Jeff asked himself.

"Red!" he shouted. "Red! Where are you?"

Suddenly he remembered the rucksack. His heart sank to his heels as he thought of the badly needed items — besides the few remaining sand- wiches — that had disappeared with it, especially the map and the compass.

How could he find his way out of these vast mountains now? How long could he and Red — once they had found each other — last without food and water?

He choked back tears as he rose to his feet

and looked up at the thick forest that loomed ahead of him. For the first time since he had run away from camp he felt hopelessly lost. He had depended on the map and the compass; they were gone now, as were his flashlight, matches, first-aid kit, wire to make snares and fishhooks out of, and the knife.

One thing was sure: he could not afford to *guess* which was north, south, east, and west. He had to be certain, or he might never get out of the mountains alive.

"Red!" he yelled again. "You big, dumb animal, where did you go?"

Jeff walked along the shoreline, his feet practically dragging from exhaustion, his clothes dripping wet.

He noticed now a bend in the river behind him. He had been too caught up in trying to save his life to have noticed it before. Red could be around the other side of it.

He trudged on, went around the bend, and there he saw the big horse standing on shore, nibbling at the grass.

"Lots you care about what happened to *me*," Jeff said out loud.

Red heard him, for he raised his head and

looked at Jeff. His right ear jerked as if a fly had lighted on it. A thigh muscle quivered.

Jeff looked him over, saw thankfully that Red had suffered no visible bruises, then mounted him.

"Okay, Red," he said. "We're on our own now. It's just you, me, and the mountains."

He looked up at the clearing sky. From the sun he judged it might be about ten or ten-thirty in the morning. Thick mounds of clouds moved like silent ships across the vast sea of blue. Soon the sun blazed from behind a cloud, and Jeff took a mental fix. He knew the sun rose in the east, so a northwesterly direction would be back over his left shoulder as he faced the sun. He would inevitably be a few degrees off his course, but he had to move on just the same.

They rode straight ahead. If they were lucky, they should see the Azure Mountains sometime that afternoon.

Then Jeff looked again at the river. A sudden thought made him cry out with delight. Why not follow it? he thought. It must be the St. Regis, and, if his memory served him correctly, the map showed that it flowed in a northwesterly direction. Somewhere on that river there must be a town. He had some money, enough to buy himself and Red something to eat. Then he could ride back into the woods before someone saw him and got suspicious.

He took up Red's reins and steered the horse along the riverbank. The sun was back over his right shoulder; he was almost certain that he was heading in the right direction.

After traveling about two miles, he became aware that his clothes had practically dried. He found berries growing in the thicket, and ate them to help satisfy his growing hunger.

He remembered reading about strawberries growing best in the sun, and at last came upon several patches of them, which he shared with his horse.

Farther on he came upon a scene that made him draw Red to a halt. A long-billed, black-headed loon was standing in the water, a small chick resting on its back. Jeff waited breathlessly. It was a heart-warming sight he could never expect to see again.

Suddenly the mother's white-ringed neck swooped downward, and her head disappeared into the water. A second later it reappeared, with a fish caught in her bill.

Jeff smiled. "Look at that, Red!" he cried elatedly. "She's an expert fisherman!"

They rode on, unintentionally scaring off the loons. The chick took off first, followed by its mother. Their fast flapping wings soon lifted them over the trees and out of sight.

After a while they came upon two deer drinking at the edge of the water, a buck and a doe. Both raised their heads almost at once and peered in surprise at the newcomers for a long minute before sprinting off into the woods.

It was about an hour later when a new and surprising smell wafted across Jeff's nostrils. At the same time he saw what he thought was smoke, and for a moment he feared the worst. Maybe a forest fire had started — the kind of fire that swept through acres and acres of trees, burning to black stumps and cinders everything in its path.

But then a new smell brought with it the promise of something much more welcome.

Food.

Someone not far away had a cooking fire going.

SEVEN

In a matter of hours the giant, now fully awake, would strike.

Jeff couldn't decide. Should he ride on and avoid whoever was doing the cooking, or search out the person? Who else would be here deep in the heart of the Adirondacks? One of those grizzled old men he had read about? An old hermit who had gotten tired of civilization and gone to finish out the remainder of his life with wild animals?

Or were these hunters, with a cabin they came to every year about this time to spend their vacation?

"Hi."

The sound of a voice startled Jeff, and even Red jerked in surprise. Although Jeff had suspected that a human being was somewhere near, he really hadn't expected to meet up with anyone. When he turned around, he saw that it was a kid who had spoken, a boy younger than himself by at least three or four years.

"Hi," Jeff answered, and quickly took in the boy's dark pants and shirt, the rugged shoes, and finally his large blue eyes, which shone brightly in his round peach-colored face.

"You alone?" the boy asked, looking around.

"Yes. Well, it's just me and my horse, Red."

The smell of the fire and whatever was cooking on it began to sharpen Jeff's hunger pangs more and more. He guessed it must be around noon, and that the boy's parents were cooking lunch.

"We're going to be eating in a minute. If you're hungry, you can eat with us."

That's what he was hoping the boy would say. Instead, the boy said, "You mean to tell me that you're traveling all by yourself?"

"That's right," Jeff replied. He glanced briefly down the river toward where the smoke and the delicious odor of cooking food was coming from, hoping the kid would get the point.

54

But either the boy didn't get it, or he pretended not to. He seemed determined to pump Jeff a little further.

"You must be an extraordinary person," the boy said, stepping a little closer to get a better view of Jeff. "I would think that even an adult would think twice before going through these mountains on a horse. And with no supplies, either. Anyway, I'm sure my parents wouldn't let me do it."

Jeff shrugged. *If you only knew*, he thought.

"You're not lost, are you?" the boy asked.

"No," said Jeff. "I'm not lost. I'm just on my own, that's all."

He jerked on a rein and prodded Red gently in the ribs. "Sorry," he said. "But I've got to get going."

"Wait a minute," the boy called as Jeff and Red moved off.

Jeff pulled on the reins, looked back over his shoulder. The boy was running up behind him.

"We're having lunch soon," he said. "Why don't you join us? I'm sure my parents would be glad to have you."

Jeff hesitated. At last! But then an awful

56

thought came into his head. He was sure that there was a search party out looking for him — how long before they'd find this place? Even without a map and compass he still preferred to risk the rest of the journey home. He wanted no part of being "rescued."

"Aren't you hungry?" the boy persisted.

"Yes. But I don't want to intrude," said Jeff.

"I'm inviting you," the boy said. "So that wouldn't be intruding, would it?"

Jeff shrugged, and decided to give in. "Okay. But I can't hang around too long," he said.

The boy smiled, flashing white teeth and a space where a tooth was missing. "My name is Alan Fenwick. What's yours?" he asked.

"Jeff Belno."

"Glad to meet you, Jeff. Well, follow me."

Alan had started to run ahead of Jeff and Red when a yell resounded through the woods.

"A—lannn!"

"I'm coming!" the boy shouted back.

They had hardly gone more than fifty feet when a girl appeared out of the woods, a pink band around her head of thick blond hair. She looked a couple of years older than Alan, and so much like him there was no mistaking their relationship. Her blue jeans, torn on one knee, came to just above her ankles.

She stopped abruptly and stared at Jeff and Red as if the last thing she expected was to see another human being and a horse in this part of the world. Her mouth popped open and her eyes widened, and for a moment she stood like that, transfixed.

"Marge, this is Jeff Belno," said Alan. "This is my sister, Margaret, Jeff."

"Hi," said Jeff.

"Hi," Marge replied.

"I invited him to have lunch with us," Alan went on. "Is it ready?"

She nodded. By now she seemed to have gotten her wits together again, except for the wide-eyed attention she was giving the horse. Jeff knew the sign. He had seen it before in kids who loved horses. His own expression must have been like that when he had first laid eyes on Red.

By now Alan had started off again, and Jeff, touching Red lightly in the ribs with the heels of his shoes, followed him.

Soon they came to a thick curtain of trees growing on a finger of land that projected out into the river. Jeff saw smoke coming out from behind the trees.

He had Red follow Alan between the trees to the other side, and there he saw a man watching over a couple of pans cooking on a grate in a fireplace, and a woman setting a small picnic table. Both of them were wearing Bermuda shorts and thin jerseys. In the woods behind them was a log cabin. A couple of its windows were cracked, and one of the other panes had been replaced by a piece of cardboard. Much of the bark on the cabin had been worn off through time and harsh winter storms, but its shingled roof looked solid. Jeff thought it looked as good as any of the cabins back at Camp Ga-wan-da.

Alan began the introductions even before Jeff had drawn up close. Jeff wasn't sure whether or not he should dismount before getting a formal invitation from Alan's parents for lunch, so he stayed on his horse. He felt awkward and nervous, and somewhat hesitant about staying as once again he thought about the search for him that must be on.

Also, there would be questions. He could

either answer them and eat (if he were invited to eat), or he could ride on and not eat. Maybe starve.

But within a few moments the surprised looks on the faces of the two older Fenwicks turned to plain friendliness as they seconded Alan's invitation to Jeff to stay for a meal.

"You've got a beautiful horse, Jeff," added Mr. Fenwick, whose sun-reddened neck indicated he spent a lot of time outdoors. "Why don't you tie him up to that tree there? He'll be close enough to the water in case he wants a drink now and then."

Jeff took Mr. Fenwick's suggestion. A few minutes later they were all seated around the table, Jeff next to Alan and Margaret on one side, the older Fenwicks on the other.

Fish and chips — the fish, rainbow trout, caught within the last two hours, according to Mr. Fenwick — with pickles, peas, and mountain berries, made up the lunch, with coffee for the grownups and milk for the children.

Jeff could hardly wait for the Fenwicks to finish saying grace so that he could start eating. He thought it was odd that they should say grace at the noon meal, because in his own house it was said only at the evening meal. Except on Sundays, when Mom served a big fancy dinner at noon.

"Where do you live, Jeff?" Mrs. Fenwick asked, her eyes shielded by amber sunglasses.

"Dory Mills," he said.

"Oh? Where's that?"

Jeff was surprised she didn't know. Dory Mills was small, but anybody who lived around the Adirondacks would know of it. Apparently the Fenwicks lived much farther away.

"It's up north," Alan answered. "I remember seeing it on the map."

Mrs. Fenwick smiled. "I asked Jeff, not you, Alan."

"He's right," replied Jeff. "It is up north."

"You said you came from wherever you came from all by yourself," Alan said. "But you didn't say whether you were heading for home, or away from it. Which is it?"

Jeff blushed. He slowed down his eating, unable to force the food down past the lump that had suddenly formed in his throat. Alan had popped him a loaded question. Next he might ask, "*Why* did you leave wherever it was you left?"

"Never mind, Jeff," Mr. Fenwick spoke up. "That was a nosy question, and you don't have to answer it."

"Nosy?" exclaimed Alan. "What was nosy about it? I just asked —"

"We heard the question, Alan," Mr. Fenwick interrupted. "Better start eating while the meal's still warm. Okay?"

Alan nodded, but he didn't seem hurt — as far as Jeff could tell — by his father's mild reprimand.

"Why don't you tell Jeff where our permanent home is?" said Mrs. Fenwick to her children. "He might be wondering about that."

"We're from Cedarhurst, Long Island," Margaret explained. "Know where that is?"

"Well — I know where Long Island is."

"It's near the J. F. Kennedy Airport," Alan said.

"My father built this log cabin almost thirty years ago," Mr. Fenwick broke in quietly. "I was about five years old then. It took him all of one summer to build it, and ever since then we've been coming up here, a few weeks every summer in the peace and quiet of the mountains."

"Grandpa and Grandma used to come with us," said Alan. "Then Grandpa died a couple of years ago —"

"Five," corrected Margaret.

"— and Grandma didn't care about coming with us anymore, so we just come up here by ourselves now. We hike in from the nearest road, which is about ten miles away. Isn't that right, Dad?"

"Something like that," answered his father. "Anyway, the land — which is owned by my mother now — encompasses about twenty acres. Most of the land adjoining it belongs to the state."

Listening to the Fenwicks explain their own presence in the mountains was a welcome relief to Jeff. The less he was asked about himself the better. He vaguely suspected, though, that the Fenwicks might have drawn some conclusions as to why he was here. Alan's question, and Jeff's anxious reaction to it, surely had not gone unnoticed. Otherwise why would Mr. Fenwick have warned Alan to drop the subject?

"I think I better get going," said Jeff when he was finished. "Excuse me, and thanks for the lunch."

He got off the bench, picking up his plate, which still had some bread and chips on it. "I'll give this to my horse."

"Oh, why don't you stay for a while, Jeff?" Alan insisted. "As soon as we digest our lunch a little we'll go swimming. There's a spot just this side of the peninsula which is excellent for swimming, and the water's warm as toast."

Jeff grinned. For his age Alan was so confident and outgoing, even with a stranger.

"You must excuse him, Jeff," Margaret said softly. "He's been trying to sound like a teenager ever since his last birthday."

"Okay, kids," Mr. Fenwick intervened. "No remarks. But why don't you go for a swim, Jeff?" he said. "We've got extra pairs of bathing trunks. One of them should fit you."

"But I'm heading for home," said Jeff. *There*, he thought. *I've made that much clear. Now they won't have to wonder whether I'm coming or going.* "And it's a long ride," he added.

"It will take you at least a couple of days anyway, won't it?" Mr. Fenwick remarked. He raised an eyebrow, as if there was no doubt in *his* mind that it would take that long.

"At least," Jeff admitted.

Mrs. Fenwick smiled at him. "A swim would be quite refreshing, Jeff."

"Oh, please stay, Jeff," Margaret said. "We haven't seen another soul in two whole weeks. Do you know that we don't even have a radio? Neither Mom nor Dad *wants* to know what's going on in the outside world. Can you believe it?"

"Quit putting Jeff on the spot," said Mr. Fenwick. "And finish what you've got on your plate, Jeff. That is, if you can. We've got enough leftovers here to take care of your horse for a while."

"You sure?"

"Of course he's sure," cried Alan. Coming around the table, he took the plate from Jeff and put it back down in front of him. "Come on. Sit down and finish it."

Jeff looked at him, then at Mr. and Mrs. Fenwick and Margaret. They were just about the kindest people he had ever met. He felt that it was a remarkable accident that he had come across them.

Yet the feeling that he was being searched for preyed on his mind. How embarrassed he would be if he were found here by a search party!

But, he thought, *staying a few minutes longer wouldn't be such a risk, would it?* He could use a

little relaxation. That journey through the mountains was pretty trying.

A smile came to his lips as he made up his
mind. "Okay," he said, and sat down to finish
what was left on his plate.

EIGHT

Closer . . .

Mrs. Fenwick found a pair of Alan's red trunks that fitted Jeff. Not perfectly, but, at least, passably.

All five of them went swimming. Jeff began to feel glad that he had stayed, for the water was most refreshing. He had fallen into the river once, and been rained on in last night's storm, but the swim was different. There were people with him now, the friendliest people he had met in a long time.

And that Alan. *What a nosy kid,* thought Jeff.

He was so nosy that he had gone to the cabin, brought out the map and pointed out to his parents and Margaret exactly where Dory Mills was and exactly where they were camped!

"Man, Jeff!" he half shouted as he realized what Jeff was in for. "You've got a long, long way to go! And in these mountains? You really have a lot of guts. I'll tell you that, Jeff."

Jeff smiled modestly. "I don't know about that. I just know I'll make it, that's all."

"You'll have to make it, or you're dead!" exclaimed Alan.

They swam for over an hour, then toweled themselves and dressed. Jeff saw Margaret looking at Red again. She had gazed fondly at the big horse at least a dozen times since Jeff and Red had stopped here.

"Ever ride a horse?" he asked her.

"Never."

"Would you like to ride Red? He's really very gentle."

Her blue eyes lit up. "Oh, I'd love to, Jeff! Are you sure he wouldn't mind? He won't buck, or anything like that?"

Jeff grinned. "I'm sure of it. But I'll tell you

what. I'll hold onto the reins and lead him around while you sit on him. Okay?"

"That's so nice of you, Jeff! That is, if it's okay with my mother and father."

Margaret's parents were nearby, close enough to hear the conversation.

"Jeff's idea sounds good to us," Mrs. Fenwick told Margaret. "You ride the horse while Jeff hangs onto the reins."

Margaret had trouble mounting Red, until Jeff assisted by cupping his hands and letting her step up on them. A gentle shove and she was up.

He untethered Red, then led him along the shoreline and behind the cabin, where he saw, for the first time, a lawn about thirty feet square. There were wicker chairs and a table, and a hammock strung between two trees.

What a beautiful place, he thought. *A little piece of heaven*. Would his mother and father enjoy a place like this!

He glanced back at Margaret, and his own heart warmed as he saw the expression on her face. Red was more than just a horse to her. He was unreal. A dream. She couldn't believe that this was happening to her.

"Jeff," Margaret said suddenly. "Please stop a minute, will you?"

"Sure." Pulling back on the reins, he said, "Hold it, Red. Whoa."

Red halted, and Jeff looked up at Margaret.

She looked at him intently, her blue eyes wide and serious.

"I know it's not any of my business, Jeff," she said. "But I — none of us can understand why you're way out here in the mountains alone."

He looked hard at her a moment, then looked away. She was right; it wasn't any of her business. But how could he tell her that? She — her whole family — had been so nice to him.

"Well, I can see why you can't understand it," he answered finally. "But, I —" He almost blurted out the truth, then changed his mind. "I don't think I want to talk about it, Margaret."

"Okay. But Dad and Mom are real worried about you," she confessed. "Even though they haven't said anything to you, they told us that traveling through these mountains is really quite dangerous, even on a horse. And it's very easy to get lost."

"I won't get lost," he said.

"How do you know?"

He shrugged. "I just know, that's all."

"Oh, Jeff," she exclaimed. "You know that's no sensible answer."

"Maybe not," he admitted. "But now that I've started this trip I've got to finish it."

"But why make it hard for yourself? Dad can lead you back to the closest highway, and you can go on from there. He'd never forgive himself if he heard that something had happened to you in the mountains, Jeff."

Jeff shook his head. "You just don't understand, Margaret," he said, raising his voice slightly. "I've *got* to make this trip on my own. I promised myself I'd do it, and I'm not going to back out."

"Did you run away from someplace, Jeff?" she asked.

He stared at her. "Is that what your parents think?"

She nodded. "Me, too. You had it written all over your face all the time Mom and Dad were trying to talk with you, while we were eating. Of course, we could be wrong."

So they had guessed it, he thought. But they

71

had not wanted to embarrass him by asking him questions.

"If I tell you something, will you promise not to tell your parents until after I leave?" he said. " 'Cause I've got to leave, Margaret. I can't stay."

"You're not an orphan, are you, Jeff? You didn't escape from an orphanage, did you?"

He almost broke out laughing. "Oh, no. I'm not an orphan. But I — you promise not to tell?"

"I promise."

He hesitated before continuing. "I ran away from a camp. A boys' camp."

She stared at him. "Why did you do that?"

"I had to. The director of it was treating me like a — well — as if I were a stupid kid," he blurted out angrily. "Every time I did something he bawled me out. I could never do anything that would, well —" He had trouble thinking of the words he wanted to say.

"That would satisfy him?" Margaret said.

"That's right. You hit it on the head. Nothing I did satisfied him. And he let me know it, shaming me in front of all those guys. I had to get out of there, Margaret. I just had to."

He was breathing hard, and sweat was glistening on his forehead.

"You won't tell your parents about me till I leave, will you?"

She kept looking at him, as if turning over and over in her mind what he had told her. "I won't tell them," she promised.

"Thanks, Margaret." He smiled up at her. "Let's go now, okay?"

She returned his smile. "Okay."

After her ride was over, Jeff again told her that he had better leave, since time was going by fast. He was determined that nothing would change his mind this time. But something did.

"How about catching a few fish before you go, Jeff?" asked Mr. Fenwick. "We could cook them and you could have them for dinner tonight."

"Yeah!" Alan exclaimed. "That's a *great* idea!"

"Well — okay," agreed Jeff.

They fished, using worms as bait, and within an hour Jeff had caught three good-sized rainbow trout, and Mr. Fenwick had caught two. Thrilled, Jeff promised himself that catching the fish would be one of the first things he would tell his father about when he arrived home.

"You want to skin them yourself?" Mr. Fenwick asked.

Jeff shrugged. "I've never cleaned a fish," he confessed. "My father always did that."

"In that case, let me skin one for you," Mr. Fenwick offered. "Then you can do the others. Okay?"

"Okay."

Working at the picnic table, Mr. Fenwick sliced off the first trout's dorsal fin with the blade of a sharp knife, then ran the tip of the blade along the full length of the fish's belly, from gills to tail, and cleaned it out. Next he cut through the skin just behind the gills on both sides of the fish's head, and then carefully pulled up the skin with his fingertips and cautiously drew it back all the way to the tail, first on one side and then on the other.

"There," said Mr. Fenwick. "See how easy it is? One nice thing about skinning a fish is that there is no mess with scales. Here, see what you can do now. Just be careful with the knife. It's razor-sharp."

Slowly and carefully Jeff proceeded to follow the skinning technique exactly as he had seen

74

Mr. Fenwick do it. His biggest trouble was holding the fish still because of its sliminess. However, under the watchful eye and coaching of Mr. Fenwick, he succeeded in cutting out the dorsal fin and then slitting the fish's belly. In a few minutes he had the fish skinned. Even though he knew he had taken about four times as long as Mr. Fenwick had, he had learned something new — something else he could tell his father about.

Mr. Fenwick hadn't yelled at him, either, as Norman Dorg would have. He was patient, understanding. Wouldn't it have been great to have had *him* at camp?

After they'd skinned and cleaned out all five fish, Mr. Fenwick built a fire in the fireplace. While the wood burned down to red-hot coals, Mrs. Fenwick rolled the fish in flour. Then she greased a skillet, placed it on the grate over the fire, and laid in it the trout.

Jeff watched avidly as the grease began to sizzle and the sweet smell of the fresh fish rose from the pan. This was one of the greatest joys of camping in the woods, Jeff thought, and he was tempted to stay longer to enjoy with the Fenwicks the freedom and the pleasures of the outdoors.

But the certainty that a rescue team was on his trail made him stick to his decision to leave. Nothing could be worse than to face the humiliation of being "rescued" now.

NINE

Like a rattlesnake, it struck....

When the fish were cooked, Mrs. Fenwick wrapped them up in aluminum foil and handed them over to Jeff.

"Dad," said Alan suddenly. "Can I give Jeff my knapsack? He needs it worse than I do."

Mr. Fenwick looked at him, considered the suggestion, and nodded. "Okay. Go get it."

Alan dashed into the cabin and came back out with a knapsack that had a short, wide shoulder strap. It looked worn, but it was more than ample for the package of fish.

Mrs. Fenwick stuck the package into it, then

Mr. Fenwick added a few slices of bread, which he had also wrapped in aluminum foil.

Margaret slipped in a couple of apples and a pear, and Alan squeezed in two oranges. Jeff was about to leave when Mr. Fenwick detained him again for another minute. He went into the cabin and brought out a quart-size Thermos.

Before handing it up to Jeff, who was already astride Red, Mr. Fenwick said, "It's a long way to Dory Mills, Jeff, even by way of the river. And walking along the shore can be mighty treacherous at times. I'd gladly lead you back to the road where you can get on the highway. It would be a lot safer all around."

"You're very good to suggest that, Mr. Fenwick," Jeff said appreciatively. "But, really, I'll be all right. I won't have any trouble. I know I won't."

"Why don't you take our map?" Alan offered.

Jeff looked at him hopefully. Even without a compass he would have a fairly good idea of his route if he had a map.

"Well, if he's going along the river he really won't need it," Mr. Fenwick said. "And I'm sure that Jeff would want to think twice before attempting to head straight over the mountains."

He was peering at the forest behind him as he said it, the thick, virgin forest that spread out for many miles in every direction. There were no roads that led north, at least none that were less than twenty-five or thirty miles away. To find a road north could take more than two days on horseback.

But Jeff was adamant. "My dad and I used to hunt the mountains a lot," he said. "It isn't that I've never been in the woods before. Well, good-bye. And thanks again."

"Wait, Jeff," said Alan. "Can I get him the map, Dad?"

"Okay. I suppose it would help. I'm sorry I don't have a compass, Jeff."

"That's okay, Mr. Fenwick. A map will be a big help."

While Alan ran to the cabin to fetch the map, Mr. Fenwick handed the Thermos to Jeff.

"There's a quart of good cold milk in there," he said. "Just drink a little of it once in a while. Make it last as long as you can."

"I will, sir. Thanks."

Alan returned with the map. Then Margaret handed Jeff a folded slip of paper.

"This is our address in Cedarhurst," she said.

"Write to us in a couple of weeks. By then we'll be back home."

"I'll do that," he promised. They were so friendly — so kind. "Good-bye."

He yanked on a rein and headed Red up the river. Just before he started through the trees at the neck of the peninsula he turned and waved to them. They waved back.

About a half-mile farther on he stopped and studied the map. He found the St. Regis River, a blue line wiggling northwestward, but it was too far west in relation to Dory Mills. Not only would the trip be farther by following the river, but the chance that a rescue team would find him would be much greater.

He didn't want to be found. He had gone safely almost a third of the way; there was no reason why the remaining two thirds should be any tougher.

He would have to head more northward in an almost direct path to Dory Mills. Of course he didn't expect the path to be in a straight line. But a few miles one side of Dory Mills or the other was close enough. He'd be in familiar territory then.

He folded up the map, stuck it behind his belt,

and reined Red into the woods. In a little while the sound of the river diminished to nothing behind him.

Now and then he glanced back over his shoulder at the sun as it blazed behind the trees. It was to his left, swinging slowly westward. As long as it stayed there he knew that he was traveling in a fairly accurate direction. Sometime, perhaps before nightfall, he should catch sight of the Azure Mountains.

The trees seemed to get thicker, the going rougher. At this rate, he thought, it would take him a week to get home — if he hadn't starved by then.

He was surprised when he came upon a stream. It wasn't shown on the map, perhaps because it was so small. He decided to follow it for a while, for it seemed to flow from the direction in which he was headed.

Soon Jeff made a surprising discovery, something he had never seen before — a family of beavers.

He halted Red and watched them for several minutes as one or two would crawl upon a pile of sticks — their own manufactured dam — and chew on fish they had caught, while another two or three disappeared beneath the dam, appeared for a few moments for a surface swim, then disappeared again. The sight was a close look at how this family of beavers spent a part of its life, and Jeff wished he could stay longer to watch it. But he couldn't; he had to plod on.

He didn't know how long he had been riding when Red stopped suddenly, causing Jeff to jerk forward in the saddle. A movement on the ground caught Jeff's eye, and just a few feet ahead he saw a porcupine, its eyes glaring sharply up at Red, its quills erect.

"You don't want to mess with him, Red," Jeff cautioned. "Those quills are bad business."

He reined Red around a bush, skirting the small, bulky animal, while its alert, intent eyes watched every move the horse made.

Farther on he came upon trees with bark that looked gnawed or chewed. In a closer look, Jeff recognized the trees as beeches, and he remembered the one he had seen early this morning which the bear had considered climbing.

These beeches were broader, at least fifteen inches across, and undoubtedly laden with beech-nuts when they were in season. There were plain signs that bears had feasted on them more than once.

Hunger gnawed in Jeff's stomach more and more. But it wasn't till twilight that he decided to stop and eat. He ate two of the fish and rewrapped the other three for tomorrow. A few gulps of milk satisfied his thirst. He let Red graze on the berries and weeds that grew nearby.

He checked the map and rode till it was too dark to see, then stopped for the night.

He arose early the next morning, finding Red already awake and grazing lazily.

Jeff considered building a fire, but decided against it when he realized that the smoke would reveal his position. He had no idea how far behind him the rescue teams were, but there was a good chance that at least one of the teams had found the Fenwicks' cabin and had been told which direction Jeff had taken.

He ate another fish. Though it was cold, it tasted delicious. *The Fenwicks were real nice*, he thought. *I wonder what Mr. and Mrs. Fenwick said when Margaret told them about me.*

He drank half a cup of milk, then stuck the

Thermos into the knapsack. Next, he took out the map and studied it for a few minutes. When he had a clear idea of his route, he slipped the map back behind his belt, climbed up on Red, and rode on.

A wind started to blow, coming up so quickly that Jeff hadn't realized it till he began to hear it whistling through the trees, and saw the tops of the trees bending. He looked up at the sky. It was clear, except for some white clouds tumbling by.

In a short while, he came to a ravine, and let Red drink from the narrow stream.

Suddenly the wind picked up in intensity, howling up through the ravine and ripping off some of the slimmer branches of the trees.

Jeff shivered.

"Feels like a storm coming up, Red," he said aloud, glancing up at the sky again. "But I don't see any thunderheads, and it doesn't look like rain. Maybe it's just a big windstorm."

He had hardly gotten the words out of his mouth when he felt the ground shake. Red stopped in his tracks and whinnied.

"What was that, Red?" Jeff said nervously.

Then the earth moved again. Terror gripped

84

Jeff as he felt it trembling more each second, coupled with a sound that began as a distant roar.

Nerves tightening up like steel, Jeff listened to the roar grow louder and louder, like a thousand multiengined airplanes warming up for takeoff. And, as the sound intensified, so did the movement of the earth.

TEN

Magnitude on the Richter scale, 6.5: panic. Total destruction of unstable structures. Considerable damage to stable structures. Collapse of foundations. Ground cracked.

"It's an earthquake, Red!" Jeff cried, terror gripping him like a thousand fingers. "But it can't be!"

The earth was trembling, creating a roar that was almost unbearable. The trees shook, and moved with the earth. Bushes quivered, jerked. Animals bolted from their hiding places. Birds shrieked. The world had suddenly turned into a wild, squirming thing.

Terrified, Red let out a piercing neigh and started to run into the woods. He took a dozen long strides, then lost his balance and fell as the earth heaved and rolled like an angry sea. He screamed, caught in a web of fear.

Jeff fell off him, striking the moving ground. He felt the earth giving way underneath him, slowly at first, then gradually picking up momentum. Eyes glazed with terror, he searched frantically for something to grab, and saw a young tree an arm's length behind him.

He started to scramble up it when he felt it sway as if it might topple. Quickly he wriggled around to the other side to save himself from being crushed underneath it. Just then, from the corner of his eye he saw Red slip on his side into the ravine, his four legs churning the air in a frantic effort to regain his balance. Never in his life had Jeff seen fear in Red's eyes as he saw it then.

Red managed to stand up again. Then, letting out another terrified cry, he bolted down the ravine in desperation, trying to flee from the terrible thing that was happening.

"Red!" Jeff shouted, tears filling his throat. "Red, come back!"

Red ran on.

Suddenly the tree Jeff was clinging to sank; the earth had cracked open beneath it. He shut his eyes as loose earth showered on him, and when he opened his eyes again he saw nothing but utter darkness.

He realized he could still breathe, but he was sure that death was only minutes away.

At the Seismological Laboratory near White-face Mountain, one of several similar laboratories scattered throughout the state, Vincent Beardsley stared wide-eyed and incredulous at the readings of the cylindrical instrument in front of him. They told him that an earthquake, with a shock inten-

sity of six point five on the Richter scale, had just taken place, *and that the epicenter was somewhere in the heart of the Adirondacks!*

"Incredible!" he cried, his voice echoing against the walls of the big wood-frame building. "It's a giant!"

It took him several minutes to settle his nerves.

He recorded the time when the tremors had started: 4:58. And when they ended: 5:06. A period of eight minutes — eight minutes, during which time severe damage and possibly death to people, livestock, and wild animals could have resulted.

He took a deep breath and went to the teletype machine to report the information to the data

89

center in Rockville, Maryland, the global earthquake headquarters. Other stations registering the quake would do the same thing. Armed with all the information collected this way, the seismologists at the data center could just about pinpoint the epicenter of the quake. In minutes this information would then be sent to all the news services, radio and television stations, the Red Cross, weather bureaus, and dozens of other agencies in the United States and overseas.

"And just yesterday I thought how quiet things were around here," Vince said aloud to himself.

Some twenty-five miles south, the Search and Rescue teams, headed up by Lou Aldon, had felt the shock of the earthquake. The teams had slept in the forest through the night and had just awakened to continue the search when the quake had struck. A few minutes later, Lou was radioing Tom Murray, the district forest ranger in Watertown.

"Lou," Tom said, as he heard Aldon's voice over the telephone, "you don't know how good it is to hear your voice. How serious was the earthquake there?"

"That rattle you hear is my bones," replied Lou. "I was here in 1971 when we experienced a quake, but it was nowhere as big as this one. I've never seen guys — me included — climb trees so fast in my life. We had to, to save ourselves from dropping into the earth."

"That bad, huh?"

"You better believe it. Anyhow, all we got was a good shaking up, that's all. You know what's scaring me to death, though?"

"The runaway kid."

"Right."

"I'll give Vince Beardsley a call and ask him how serious that quake was in the mountains."

"I've got a good idea," said Lou. "Ask him what the readings were on the Richter scale, and let me know, will you?"

"Roger. Ten four."

Tom hung up, then dialed a number he had memorized long ago. After two rings he heard Vince Beardsley's soft, somewhat nervous voice.

"Hello?"

"Vince, this is Tom Murray. You okay?"

A forced chuckle came over the wire. "My

voice shows it, does it? Yes, I'm okay. That was a heck of a quake, you know."

"Yes, I figured it was," answered Tom. "Where did it hit the hardest, and how serious was it?"

"The epicenter was a few miles west of the Azure Mountains," explained Vince. "According to my readings the figures showed a magnitude of six point five on the Richter scale."

"Wow. That's high."

"It sure is. Damage could be extremely serious. Cracked earth. Crumbling buildings. Twisted rails. Broken pipes."

"How about a kid riding a horse in the mountains?"

There was a brief pause at the other end of the wire. "I'd give him a forty-sixty chance."

"You figure the odds are against his surviving it?"

"I could be wrong. I hope so. You're talking about that Belno kid who ran away from a boys' camp. I heard about it on the radio."

"That's right. Okay, Vince. Thanks."

Tom hung up, his palms sweaty. Then he dialed Lou Aldon. His nerves still unsettled, he related what Vince had told him.

Jeff lay trapped underground, yet he was breathing. And he knew that as long as he could breathe he would live. But how long could he last?

He tried forcing his hands out along the tree, hoping to pull himself out. The earth was cold, damp, and heavy around him. Pushing his hands through it took all the muscle he had.

Gradually he inched his hands forward, then his body. Suddenly he thought: *What if the whole tree is buried?*

His heart seemed ready to explode, pounding so hard he could hear it. But how would he survive if he didn't try? He *had* to try!

He moved forward an inch, and then another. He had no idea which way the tree was slanting. He could be burrowing himself deeper into the earth for all he knew.

Suddenly he stopped, realizing that he could move his fingers freely!

Now his whole hand was above the ground!

Excitement welled up in him as he struggled with all his might to creep farther up toward the surface. Some dirt had gotten into his nostrils and his mouth. He spat, and blew out through his nose.

Then his head was out of the ground, and joy spilled over in his heart as he saw daylight again.

He dragged himself the rest of the way out of the ground, wiped the dirt off his face and out of his ears, and looked for Red.

The horse was nowhere in sight.

ELEVEN

About a hundred yards away, Red was half buried in the ravine, with water washing over his back and neck. Although his hind legs were almost completely buried, his forelegs were free; he was struggling desperately to pull himself out.

At first, as he dug his hooves hard into the earth beneath the fast-flowing water, they only churned the ground, turning it into mud.

Eventually, though, the mud wore away, and his hooves came down against the hard rock underneath. The muscles in his neck and shoulders bulging, he pushed against the rock and began to force his legs out of the ground. Little by little

he worked himself free, and then he was out, snapping his tail in a gesture of victory.

He shook himself, and again whipped his tail around to brush off the dirt from his red, velvety coat. He stretched his neck, shook the loose dirt from his mane, and uttered a triumphant, whinnying cry that carried up through the ravine and for hundreds of yards around.

Then he stood still and looked around. The uprooted trees and jutting boulders left by the earthquake were of little concern to him. He was confused, though. His earlier fears had left him, but the boy wasn't around to tell him what to do.

Gingerly, he stepped out of the water and started to climb up the shallow rise of the mountain. He leaped over a fallen tree, skirted bushes, brushed against prickly vines. The rising sun, filtering through the trees, began slowly to dry the mud on his coat to hard, crusty patches.

Suddenly he heard a cry some distance away. He stood still, his head held high, his ears erect.

The cry came again. It was a familiar voice, and Red lowered his head, shook it and whinnied. Then he plunged ahead, leaping over small, young trees that clung to the earth by a few twisted roots.

"Red!"

The voice was much closer now, and the horse ran on.

When they saw each other, Red raced forward and let out another whinny before drawing up short before the boy and nuzzling him.

"Oh, Red!" Jeff cried happily. "Am I glad you're all right!"

Up in Dory Mills, which had felt the shock from the earthquake (although some of the people merely thought that workmen were blasting rock in the mountains to open up a new road), Mrs. Belno heard the news over the small kitchen radio.

"That shock you felt earlier this morning was actually an earthquake," reported the announcer. "The epicenter of the quake was in the vicinity of the Azure Mountains. So far no serious damage to dams has been reported, nor loss of life."

Ann Belno was on her feet before the announcer had finished the sentence.

"It *was* an earthquake!" she cried, looking across at her husband sitting in the armchair by the porch window. "It *was!* I had a feeling! Jeff could have been hurt in it, John!"

John stared at her, his cheeks pale. "All right, all right. Take it easy," he said.

"Take it easy? Jeff is in those mountains, John! How can I take it easy? How can *you* take it easy?"

"Now, look. You know I don't mean it quite that way. I'm just trying to keep myself under control, and that's what I'm trying to tell you to do. You heard the announcer. No serious damage has been reported, nor loss of life. Jeff could be safe."

"Could be. But we don't *know*."

"No, we don't know. But we can't expect the worst, Ann. We'll go crazy if we do. We'll just have to wait."

He looked away from her and stared at the floor, his hands gripping the edges of the chair. Ann knew he was as worried as she was.

"Those Search and Rescue men," she went on anxiously. "They might have been caught in it, too."

"They might have," he said, without looking up at her. "But you've got to remember that if the earthquake was a severe one — a real severe one — we would have suffered some damages."

"Maybe we have," replied his wife. "Maybe we have and don't know about it yet. Dory Mills isn't a big town. And it's old. Some of the houses are very old. It wouldn't take much to knock them down."

John looked up, his eyes shiny. "We would have heard about it, Ann. That announcer would have reported it. Listen to me. It wasn't that serious. Can you understand that? It wasn't that serious."

He looked back at the floor.

She tried to understand, but it wasn't easy. "I love that son of ours, John," she said. "I love him very much."

"So do I," John said. "He's a good boy. A very good boy."

"If something happened to him . . ." Ann couldn't finish what she wanted to say, and choked back tears.

John got up, went to her, wiped away the tears. He tried to smile.

"Why don't you make us some coffee?" he said. "Then we'll just wait. That's about all we can do now, anyway. Okay?"

She looked at him, and nodded. For just a moment she had the strength to smile back.

It was five minutes of eleven when the phone rang in Tom Murray's office. Tom had been sitting on pins and needles for nearly six hours, had drunk eight cups of coffee, and had wondered many times why he had chosen a forest ranger's career. There had to be hundreds of other available careers that were far less demanding and nerve-racking.

Putting his ninth cup of coffee aside, noting it ripple as his hand trembled, he picked up the red phone. "Yes?"

"Tom — Lou Aldon. Got some good news and some other news."

"I love the way you put that," said Tom, only half relieved. "Give me the good news first."

"Right. Most of the guys on the Search and Rescue team got through the quake without a scratch," said Lou. "Some got cuts and bruises, but nothing very serious."

"Thank God," said Tom. "Now the other news."

"Okay. We found a family of four — husband

and wife and two kids — somewhat bruised and shaken up from the quake. But that's all."

"What do you mean, 'But that's all'?"

"Well, we still haven't found the Belno boy," said Lou.

TWELVE

A loon, standing like a sentinel in shallow water, jerked its small head around and surveyed the scenery in silence. A bluejay called from its perch high up on a spruce tree. Still higher, a hawk glided effortlessly in a wide circle, its sharp eyes watching for prey.

On the bank of the river, newly widened by a small lake that had burst a few miles above it, Jeff and Red were resting after their ordeal. Jeff was busy knotting a piece of his torn shirt over a cut just above his left elbow.

"Guess we're lucky, Red. We're real lucky," he said.

Red was lying on his side. He lifted his head at

the sound of Jeff's voice, and rolled his huge brown eyes toward the boy. There was a bruise on his muzzle, and several scratches on his belly and back.

Jeff wondered how widespread the effects of the earthquake were. Had it damaged other parts of the mountains very much? Had it affected Camp Ga-wan-da? Were any of the guys hurt?

Then he thought of his mother and father and Patty Marie up in Dory Mills. Had the earthquake been severe enough to have affected them?

Please, God, make them be okay. Make them all be okay. The people, too. Everybody.

Jeff's thoughts then turned to another worry — his running away. He began to think about why he'd done it, what his *real* reasons had been.

He lay back, the dry leaves and needles like a soft bed under him.

Was it really Tommy Botner's fault? he asked himself. Tommy had been at Camp Ga-wan-da the year before and had described it as a nice place to spend two weeks — except for the camp director, Norman Dorg.

"You won't like him," Tommy had said. "He's strict, and tougher than any teacher you ever saw. He chewed me out twice for being late for chow.

And he made me do ten stinking pushups for nothing. Just for nothing!"

Jeff wondered now what that *nothing* had been. "But it must have been something, Red," Jeff said out loud. "Mr. Dorg wouldn't make a kid do ten pushups for no reason at all."

Then he asked himself: *Why didn't I think of all this before? I believed everything that Tommy told me! That must be why I told Dad I wouldn't go to the camp unless I could have Red there with me. I was expecting trouble. I had a suspicion all the time that something would happen with Norm Dorg that would make me want to run away from the place.*

A lump formed in his throat. *I was wrong*, he told himself. *I shouldn't have believed all that stuff that Tommy had told me. I should have gone to camp and taken things in stride just like all the other kids. No matter what my reasons are, Mom and Dad surely can't be proud of me when they heard their son had run away from camp.*

He rose, leaving an impression of his body on the matted leaves and needles.

"Come on, Red," he said, happy that his mind was made up. "We're heading back down the river. We're going back to Camp Ga-wan-da. If

Mr. Norman Dorg wants to chew me out for running away, let him. I'll even do *twenty* stinking pushups!"

At Jeff's signal Red scrambled to his feet, and both horse and boy started down the river, sticking close to the southern shore.

In the sky, the wily hawk continued to watch the earth below for any small prey that happened along.

Sometime later Jeff heard a familiar droning sound.

"Red!" he cried. "It sounds like a helicopter!"

The sound grew louder, and Jeff pulled Red up close to the water's edge, this time anxious to be seen.

"Here!" he shouted, waving, for it was a helicopter. It was flying into his line of vision. "Here we are! Here!"

But the helicopter flew on, vanishing behind the trees.

"Come back!" Jeff cried desperately. "Oh, please, come back!"

As the helicopter moved out of sight, Jeff swallowed the lump that had risen in his throat. He

was ready to give up hope when suddenly, the sound came again. It grew louder.

"It's coming back!" Jeff shouted.

He waited, hoping. There it was! Frantically, he started waving again.

"We're here! Here!"

The helicopter flew over the trees, straightened its course over the river, then seemed to pause in midair for a few seconds before dropping down closer.

Soon Jeff was able to see the two-man crew. Then the man on the passenger side leaned out, waved to him, and called through a megaphone: "Stay put, Jeff! A rescue team will be here in about an hour! It's good to see you, Jeff!"

Tears dimmed Jeff's eyes. "It's good to see you, too!" he answered.

THIRTEEN

Late that afternoon, as dusk approached, and all
the news reporters, photographers, and curiosity-
seekers left Camp Ga-wan-da, Jeff sat on the
shore of Pointed Rock Pond next to his mother
and father and Patty Marie. At his left sat
Norman Dorg, a tall, strapping man whose eyes
looked somewhat sad and tired from an ordeal
that had lasted almost three days.

"I think I learned something from this," he
said in a quiet, thoughtful voice. "Looking back
now, I can see that I might have been a little too
tough on some of the kids. I have no excuse for
that, except that I've always believed in a certain

amount of discipline. If you think that I'm responsible for what Jeff did, and you —"

"Now, wait a minute, Mr. Dorg," John Belno interrupted. "You had a job to do and you did it. You heard what Jeff said. He got a little carried away. He came back to tell you that, and to finish his stay."

"I know." Norman Dorg smiled. He looked at Jeff. "I really appreciate that, Jeff."

"Thanks, Mr. Dorg."

"If there are medals to be given out for survival methods, you certainly should get one," Norman Dorg said. "I'm sure that you learned more from your escapade in the mountains than you would ever have learned from me."

Jeff thought about the berries that had helped him through a spell of hunger, of the water he had boiled to make it safe to drink, and of meeting up with the Fenwicks. He hadn't told his father yet about skinning rainbow trout, but he had plenty of time for that later.

"Has anybody heard about the Fenwicks?" he asked curiously.

"That family you spent some time with?" said Dorg. He nodded. "Their cabin suffered some damage, but the family came out of it okay. Oh, a few bruises, but nothing real serious."

"I'm glad to hear that," said Jeff. "They were so nice to me. They didn't want me to leave, you know."

"So we heard," said Dorg.

The sound of a whinny came from behind them. Jeff and the others turned to look at Red, who was standing in the open horse van hitched to the rear of Mr. Belno's car. He was looking back at them.

"You really didn't have to ask your parents to take Red back home, you know," Dorg told Jeff. "I would have let you keep him company a couple of hours a day."

"I thought it would be better if Mom and Dad took him home," Jeff answered.

"Okay," said Dorg. "That's up to you."

Red whinnied again, and Jeff got up. "I'll be right back," he said, and ran to the van.

His heart pounded as he stopped in front of it, and his eyes glistened.

"I'm going to miss you, Red," he said softly. "We went through a lot together during these last few days. An awful lot."